To Antonia and Rosie - J.S
To Mum, Dad and James. You know you're in it! - M.W

THAT PESKY DRAGON

by Julie Sykes and Melanie Williamson

First published in hardback in 2007
This paperback edition published in 2008
by Hodder Children's Books

Hodder Children's Books
338 Euston Road
London NW1 3BH

Hodder Children's Books Australia
Level 17/207 Kent Street
Sydney, NSW 2000

ISBN: 978 0 340 93200 1

Printed in China

Hodder Children's Books is a
division of Hachette Children's Books.
An Hachette Livre UK Company
www.hachettelivre.co.uk

That Pesky Dragon

Written by
Julie
Sykes

Illustrated by
Melanie
Williamson

Hodder Children's Books

A division of Hachette Children's Books

IZZY'S DAD HAD A FARM.

And on that farm there was a herd of cows…

a goat…

a flock of sheep…

a brood of hens...

three cats...

two dogs...

and a dragon!

It didn't take everyone long to realise that there was a dragon on the farm; its fierce roar soon gave it away! When Izzy stood on tiptoes and peered out of her bedroom window, she could just see the tip of the dragon's tail on top of the hill by the well.

Rrrrooooaaaarrrr!

'Can we go and look at it?' asked Izzy.

'Certainly not,' said Dad. 'Dragons are far too dangerous. If we leave it alone, it'll be gone by tomorrow.'

But the next morning it was the roar of the dragon
and not the cockerel that woke Izzy up from her cosy dream.

Rrrrooooaaaarrrr!

'It's still here then,' thought Izzy, secretly pleased.
But she was in for a shock when she went out into the cold
to collect the eggs for breakfast.

'These eggs feel rock hard,' said Izzy as she shivered her way around the hen house.

'It's that pesky dragon,' said Grandpa, angrily. 'His fiery breath has hardboiled the eggs!'

Izzy was desperate to go and look at the dragon, but Mum wouldn't hear of it.

'That dragon's a mean one. You can tell from its roar,' she said.

Rrrrroooaaaarrrr!

'I think it sounds sad,'
said Izzy. 'Can't I have
a tiny peek?'

'Definitely not,'
said Mum. 'Go indoors
and with luck it'll fly
away soon.'

But the dragon didn't fly away.

That afternoon when Izzy went outside to help Mum milk the cows, they were in for another shock.

'Yoghurt!' cried Izzy.

'Oh dear,' said Mum. 'It's that pesky dragon's fault. Its roaring has scared the cows and turned their milk to yoghurt!'

Rrrrooooaaaarrrr!

The next morning it was the light of the dragon's fiery breath and not the light of the rising sun that woke Izzy. A lovely smell was drifting up the stairs.

'Mmm, toast,' cried Izzy, sliding down the banister.

'It's not toast; it's my prize wheat!'
Dad said bitterly. 'That pesky dragon
burnt a whole field in the night.
This can't go on. I'm phoning
REMOVE-A-DRAGON!'

'Not REMOVE-A-DRAGON!' shrieked Izzy.
'Why don't you just ask the dragon to leave?'

'It's far too dangerous,' said Dad, picking up the phone.
'It's fierce that dragon; just listen to its roar.'

'It sounds hurt not fierce
if you ask me,' said Izzy.
'Now run along while I
make this call,' said Dad.

Rrrrooaaaarrrr!

So Izzy ran. She ran
out of the farmhouse, past
the chicken shed, through the cow
field and all the way up the hill towards
the dragon…

Suddenly, Izzy grew scared.

What if the dragon was dangerous?

What if it was hungry?

What if it ate little girls for breakfast?

She panicked.

But it was too late.
The dragon had
already seen her.

Gulp!

Izzy took a brave
step forward – she could
see the scales on its tail and feel
the heat of its breath.
    But the big, roaring, scary dragon
was just a tiny dragon trapped
in the well, crying for help.

'I've been shouting for help for days,' the dragon cried.

Izzy ran back down the hill
and fetched Mum, Dad, Grandpa and
the REMOVE-A-DRAGON lady to help.

'They look scary,' sniffed the dragon as they tramped towards him with spades and ropes.

'Don't worry,' said Izzy. 'Sit still and don't breathe or you might singe us when we pull you out!'

The dragon held his breath while Izzy, the REMOVE-A-DRAGON lady, Mum, Dad and Grandpa pulled, and pulled, and pulled until...

Now Izzy's Dad has a farm with a herd of cows...

a flock of sheep...

a brood of hens...

three cats...

a goat...

two dogs...

and a dragon!

And Izzy loves cold mornings.
With a dragon around there's always
hot milk, hardboiled eggs and toast
for breakfast!

MILK

Other great Hodder picture books perfect to share with children:

978 0 340 91161 7

978 0 340 91779 4

978 0 340 91153 2

978 0 340 89329 6

978 0 340 93241 4   (HB)
978 0 340 93242 1   (PB)

Hodder
Children's
Books

A division of Hachette Children's Books